Degrees

of

Glory

Degrees
of
Glory

by
Richard M. Siddoway

BONNEVILLE BOOKS™

Springville, Utah

ISBN: 1-55517-686-0
e.1

Published by Bonneville Books
Imprint of Cedar Fort Inc.
www.cedarfort.com

Distributed by:

Typeset by Kristin Nelson
Cover design by Nicole Cunningham
Cover design © 2003 by Lyle Mortimer

Printed in the United States of America
10 9 8 7 6 5 4 3 2 1

Printed on acid-free paper

Library of Congress Cataloging-in-Publication Data

Siddoway, Richard M.
   Degrees of glory/ by Richard M. Siddoway.
        p. cm.
   ISBN 1-55517-686-0 (acid-free paper)
1. Mormons--Fiction. 2. Future life--Fiction. 3. Death--Fiction. I.
Title.

PS3569.I29 D44 2003
813'.54--dc21

                          2003000746

To Janice

Preface

On February 16, 1832, the prophet Joseph Smith and his counselor, Sidney Rigdon, were in the process of translating and correcting the New Testament. They were working in an upper room of the John Johnson home where Joseph, his wife, Emma, and their two adopted twins were staying. Joseph and Sidney were in the company of about a dozen other men and were working on the fifth chapter of John. As they pondered the 28th and 29th verses, the heavens opened and the Prophet and Sidney received six revelations that extended for a period of an hour or more. These revelations were collectively called the vision and are now contained in the Doctrine and Covenants as Section 76.

Eleven years later, in January of 1843, W.W. Phelps wrote a sixteen line poem dealing with life after death and dedicated it to the Prophet Joseph. A month later Joseph responded with a 78-stanza poetic rendition of the vision.

While Joseph and Sidney were receiving the vision, they were commanded to write some portions of it and, likewise, to not record other portions. Sidney, who was completely enervated by the experience, apparently stayed up much of the night completing his record of what he had witnessed. The result, Section 76, is a wonderful description of those who will reside in the various degrees of glory.

As I have read and re-read this scripture, I have often wondered what those kingdoms looked like. Section 137 of the Doctrine and Covenants has a brief description of the celestial kingdom, but, for the most part, the scriptures are singularly silent, as are the words of the prophets.

What follows, then, is a fictionalized visit as seen through the eyes of the author. I claim no great gift of prophecy and this, obviously, should not be considered as doctrine or any attempt to enlarge upon scripture. The errors, and there are bound to be many, are mine. But perhaps this simple story will strike a responsive chord. The day will come, for all of us, when we will have an opportunity to experience a more accurate representation.

Richard M. Siddoway

Chapter 1

"You've been duped! Lied to!" the man said, shaking his head and smiling a wolfish grin. "He won't come back for you. The master will see to that." He looked past me at the retreating light.

"But he said he would, when he left me at the gate," I replied as a tremor ran down my spine.

"Oh, there was a time when I'd have believed that as well, but that was long ago. But now I know that no one leaves here." He turned slowly toward the impenetrable darkness behind him. "Judas, we have another one," he called out.

Another figure, dark, gray, and brooding, walked out of the shadows toward me. "Welcome. You'll like it here." He inspected me from head to toe, his eyes nearly invisible under a beetled brow. "You're really new, aren't you?"

"New? I suppose. I'm not sure what you mean."

He shaded his eyes with his hand and squinted until they were nearly shut. "Yes, I can tell you're new, you're still so bright!"

"Bright?"

"You hurt my eyes. But, never mind, you'll fade soon enough, now that you're here." He turned to the figure who had greeted me. "Cain, why don't you show our latest member around, if you can stand the brightness."

The figure sneered. "Are you telling me what to do?"

1

"No, no, merely a suggestion." Judas withdrew a step into the darkness that surrounded us. "You know it was nothing more than that." Behind him I caught a glimpse of flittering gray.

"I'm sure. You'd do well to remember your proper place." He turned to me, "Ah, you're beginning to fade already. Would you like a tour? It's a wonderful place to be."

"It is?"

"Truly wonderful. Perfect. No one ever does anything wrong here."

"They don't?" I said incredulously.

Cain shook his head slowly. "Never. Everyone knows the master's will and follows it exactly."

"But what if they choose to do something wrong?"

"Choose?" Cain rolled the word beneath his tongue. "That's not a word I understand." He smiled thin-lipped at me. "But why would anyone want to disobey? There is order here. Complete order."

We walked slowly through the darkness, the only light being that which seemed to emanate from my body. I could see gray, indistinct shapes, mostly with my peripheral vision. When I turned my head to focus on them they seemed to melt into the darkness. Cain gestured with his hands, "They won't bother you."

"Who—what are they?"

"The wraiths, the ones who are different."

"Different?"

"The ones who've never experienced the corporal experience. You'll understand as you get used to this wonderful place. So soothing—so orderly."

The darkness seemed to draw even more closely around us as we walked. "There seem to be a lot of them."

"Oh, there are, and we wish there were more." He gestured again. "It's hard to believe that two-thirds of the host could be deceived." He shook his head, "So sad. The master tried so hard."

"But Father said—"

Cain's eyes tightened to tiny slits as he cut me off. "We don't talk about Father," he said. "Not after the betrayal."

"Betrayal?"

"When he chose the other plan and lost his power." A smile returned to his face. "Master tried so hard to keep anyone from being lost, but perhaps you remember?"

I shook my head, "What you say seems to stir vague memories, but it is as if a veil—"

"I understand," Cain replied. "Thankfully a third of them followed the master, or I suppose all would be lost."

"You have stirred a memory," I said, "a memory of weeping and wailing."

"Ah, yes," said Cain. "If you listen you can hear it now. We weep all the time for those who were deceived and followed the other son."

I listened and heard the thin, keening cry that wrapped itself around me like a transparent sheet. The darkness was becoming more complete and caressed me with an oily blackness that seemed to invade every part of my body and cloak me in stifling warmth.

Cain's smile became broader, "You're beginning to see, aren't you?"

"It's all so different than I expected," I said, straining to see the figure beside me.

3

"Well, the lies are so pervasive, I can understand why you might not be quite prepared."

I nodded my head. "Perhaps you could explain."

"Certainly." He paused a moment. "If you truly loved your children, as the master does, how could you allow any one of them to be lost? It's inconceivable, isn't it?"

"But they have their agency," I countered.

"Agency?" Cain spat the word out. "It's but an excuse for failure. You'd be wise not to use that word again." He stroked his chin. "Think of the war and pestilence, the misery and sickness that can be avoided if everyone just does what he's suppose to do. Remove agency and you remove all of these terrible calamities that need not be."

I noticed that the light around me was growing dimmer as Cain spoke. He smiled broadly at me.

"I'm sure you're beginning to see the logic in this, aren't you?"

Slowly, almost imperceptibly I nodded my head. Behind me, around me, the wraiths continued their incessant wailing. "But the sacrifice," I said. "The atonement."

"What about it?" Cain bristled.

"Doesn't it mean anything?"

The smile reappeared on Cain's face. "Of course. Without it I could not reign over the master."

"I don't understand?"

"The one good thing to come out of all of that," he dismissed it with a waive of his hand, "was this." He patted his chest with the palms of both of his hands. "A body, something the master will never have." He smiled a cold and brittle smile. "But I have. And despite the wandering, the endless wandering, ultimately I will reign as Master

Mahan over all of Gehenna." He laughed and a shiver raced up my spine. "And now that moment is nearly upon us."

The blackness closed in as if a cold, crystalline carapace were fitting itself over my face. "It is so different from what I'd been taught."

"I understand," he said soothingly. "The lies are very persuasive, aren't they? I'm just so happy you found the truth before it was too late. We must truly be vigilant or the deceit of the enemy will enslave more of our brothers and cause them to fall." The light was dimming and I could barely make out Cain's features. "It's wonderful that you have come," he said softly.

If felt as if my tongue were bound and thick darkness began to gather around me. I struggled against it and finally finding my voice, called out, "Why have you forsaken me? You said you'd come."

Through the seemingly impenetrable darkness a point of light appeared in the distance. Slowly it grew brighter and closer. Cain's face turned darker and more menacing until the Guide stood just outside the gate.

"What are you doing here?" Cain snarled.

The Guide smiled broadly, but said nothing.

"Why did you leave me here?" I asked as the fear fled from my body along with the darkness that surrounded me.

"I came when you called," the Guide said. "I always will."

"You can't have him," Cain said menacingly. "No one leaves here. This is the black hole of the universe where nothing escapes."

"He was not one of yours," said the Guide. "But he needed this experience for his own good." He smiled a gentle smile. "I have descended below all of this. You know that." Lines of sorrow crossed His brow.

"You are nothing," Cain spat. "I have known you from the beginning. Get out of my sight. You can imagine how much I hate you!"

"As you wish," whispered the Guide. "You can't imagine how much I love you." Tears were streaming down His face.

"And take him with you." He pointed at me. "He doesn't seem to be a true believer." He pulled his robes around him and spun as if to vanish into the darkness. "This isn't over," he called over his shoulder.

The Guide watched as Cain disappeared into the liquid blackness and then gestured gently. "Come," He said. "Follow me."

Chapter 2

"I'm glad you called," He said.

I felt a warmth and a glow returning to my body. "Why?" I asked as I stepped beside him.

"Their arguments are persuasive, aren't they?"

"Yes, I suppose." We walked slowly and deliberately along the path. The Guide saw me shiver. "What a terrible place!" I exclaimed at last.

He nodded. "It would have been better had they never been born," He said sorrowfully and somberly. Then, "Look, we're nearly at our destination."

We were approaching a great and spacious city. Buildings extended as far as the eye could see. I could hear the noise and bustle reaching out to me. "I'll leave you here," said the Guide. "You know what to do when you're ready to leave." He smiled gently and gestured toward the city gate. I waved tentatively and entered the teeming community.

Immediately I was engulfed in a sea of people who surged down the street toward an imposing skyscraper. I was swept along, jostled and bumped rudely as the throng pushed inexorably down the street. I struggled to reach the edge of the flowing stream of bodies that moved forward as a great unstoppable tide.

"Excuse me," I said as I bumped into a tall figure beside me.

"Watch it!" he said back and gave me a not-too-gentle shove as he forced himself into a spot in front of me. The wave of bodies flowed forward until we came to the steps leading to the portal of the building. The doors glowed in bronze, ornate splendor. The building rose dozens of stories high until the top was almost lost from sight. The crowd around me jostled for position until the doors opened and three men walked onto the landing. The rude murmuring of the throng quieted as one of the men raised his hands high above his head.

"Good people," he began. It seemed his voice was amplified by some unseen means. "I—we appreciate you coming here this wonderful day. If you will make yourselves comfortable, the debate will begin in a few moments." He lowered his hands. "It's wonderful to see such participation." He turned gracefully and walked to a raised platform on one side of the portico. Slowly he ascended until he stood well above the crowded courtyard and then with a flourish of his robe sat down in the gilded chair that gave him an unobstructed view of the proceedings below. With great solemnity he rapped his scepter on the marble top of the dais.

I turned my attention to the two men who walked forward to the edge of the porch. One bowed mockingly to the other and said, "Why don't you go first, Martin?"

The other returned the bow, "Thank you, Julius." His gaze swept over the multitude below. He cleared his throat, "My good friends," he paused for effect, "and you are my friends. Before I begin, let me assure you that I feel as deeply as any of you the problems associated with the swelling number of people who are moving into our community." He raised his hands, palms forward, and shook his head slowly from side to side. "Nevertheless, they must have some place to stay. We have no right—no alternative to their coming here. I know the number is enormous. I know the fears you have within the community—Oh, yes, I hear your cries of, 'There goes the neighborhood,' and 'Build wherever you want, but not in my backyard.'" He wiped his upper lip with the back of his hand. "But the simple fact is they are coming. And they must have space. The Baten Kaitos development is nearly filled. I don't know how we'd fit anyone else into the Secunda Giedi subdivision even with a shoehorn. We just have to expand into some of the spots of unused space." A rumble went through the crowd.

"I am proposing today a great new development that would stretch between Eta Carinae and Gomeisa."

A gasp went up from the crowd.

"As with the other developments that Pollux Realty has created, this will be a planned community. There will be a mix of architectural styles and various sized homes. We will do everything in our power to make it fit in with what already exists. It is not a matter of 'build it and they will come.' They are coming and we must build."

A low rumble seemed to sweep over the crowd. Martin raised his hands above his head and waited until the noise subsided. Slowly he turned and took a seat while Julius rose to his feet.

"My dear friend Martin makes a persuasive argument for his new development. Oh, yes, very persuasive. What he left out of his description, of course, is that these new souls coming to live with us are not the final few but only the beginning of a throng as numerous as the sands of the sea. This new development of his will scarcely meet the ongoing needs of the multitude of souls."

The crowd shifted in discomfort.

"I say we need a longer range plan. We've all been there. We've all struggled with our individual problems until we were ready to arrive in this beautiful kingdom. We've all found places to settle down. But now Martin wants to make you believe that the end is in sight. That we need to absorb only a few more into our midst. Well it just isn't so. Think of a million souls. That's right. Ponder that for a minute."

He paused and folded his arms across his chest. The hem of his robe swished around his feet. "Well, my friends, it isn't just a million. It isn't just ten million. We're talking billions." He paused again for effect. "Of course the other part of this equation that Martin failed to mention is the question of control. If he's responsible for building this community, whom do you think those who come to live there will look to for guidance? To whom do you think they'll turn for leadership? To you? Of course not. To me? Not likely." He extended his hand in Martin's direction until the sleeve fell back from his robe and revealed a pointing finger. "Perhaps my dear friend Martin?"

A rumble went through the crowd again. Julius raised his hands to quell the sound. "And, my friends, if they honor Martin thus, have they not given him more power?" He paused, shook his head from side to side, and then dropped his accusing hand to his side, and returned to his seat. "Defeat his proposal. Let us form a commission who will supply us with a long range solution."

Martin lifted himself to his feet and walked forward to the edge of the platform. "Ah, Julius. Power, always power." He shook his head. "Would you rather have these souls wandering the streets homeless? Of course not! We need to provide for them so that we can absorb them into our great kingdom." He turned toward Julius. "A long-range plan? A vestige of where we use to live. You know there is no meaning to long-range. There is no past, present, or future here—there is only now. "

I turned to the man next to me. "What does he mean?"

He put his hand on my shoulder. "Wait until after they finish and I'll explain it to you." He smiled a knowing smile.

Martin resumed his argument. "Some would say there is no time to waste. In fact there is no time. These souls are upon us, as we speak. We must accommodate them." He gestured wide with his arms. "Please, I implore you, give me your vote to begin immediately." He returned to his seat.

Julius stood slowly and looked at his opponent. "Color it any way you want, my friend, it is merely an attempt to gain more power." He turned to the teeming congregation. "Don't be deceived. This is nothing but a naked grab for power. Although I must agree that we need to plan because, as the natural sifting process has gone on, we are now seeing a different sort finally make it to our kingdom." Without further comment he turned and walked quickly back toward the building. The doors opened silently at his approach and he disappeared within.

Atop the platform the figure arose from his throne, tapped his scepter on the floor and announced, "The voting will commence immediately." He descended to the floor of the portico and led Martin with him through the silent doors.

The man beside me grasped my arm as the throng began to disperse down the myriad streets that radiated from the palace in front of us. "You must be new," he said with a smile. "Please come with me." Gently he led me through the ocean of moving bodies toward another resplendent building. The door opened in front of us and we entered a beautifully appointed room. "Please, have a seat. My name is Cassius." He gestured toward a padded chair. "Perhaps something to eat?"

"That would be wonderful."

He raised his hand and the sound of a gently ringing bell was heard.

"And what might I call you?"

"My name is Mark."

When did you arrive?" he asked as a young woman entered the room bearing a tray of small sandwiches and tarts. "Please," he said, indicating the tray of food.

"Just when the crowd was going to the debate," I replied, making a selection from the proffered tray. "Thank you."

The young woman smiled at me. "My pleasure," she said softly.

"Ah, then you haven't seen the glories of this kingdom," he said, making his own selection of food. He smiled at the girl, who turned and left through a portal to my right.

"No, I haven't. But I'd like to. This place is so much friendlier than the last place I visited."

"I understand." He chewed the food slowly. "Did you understand what was going on?" He pointed toward the palace across the square.

"Some of it, I think. Apparently you're expecting an influx of people and there is some disagreement as to how they will be accommodated."

My host nodded his head. "On the surface that is what was being discussed."

"And below the surface?"

"Well, both men made their point. Martin wants to supply homes, palaces really, for those who are arriving and Julius is worried that Martin is trying to accrue more power. It isn't a new problem. Power struggles have gone on forever."

"I suppose," I replied as I finished my sandwich. "What I really didn't understand was the discussion about there being no past or future. Can you explain that to me?"

"Certainly." He drummed his fingers on his chin. "I'm going to try to explain it as simply as possible, but it still takes some getting used to."

I nodded my head. "Please."

"You are familiar with railroad trains, I guess?"

"Of course," I replied, with a nod of my head.

"Well, suppose you were seated at the side of a railroad crossing and a train had stopped in front of you." He smiled gently. "Suppose the train car in front of you was made of glass, so you could see right through the side of it. Are you with me so far?"

"Yes. So far."

"Further suppose that a steel ball was held on the ceiling of the train car by an electric magnet. And let's say the distance from the ceiling to the floor is exactly sixteen feet."

"I think I have the picture in my mind."

"Good, good. Now, on earth the attraction of gravity will make that ball take exactly one second to fall from the ceiling to the floor."

I wrinkled my brow. "If you say so."

"Well, you probably remember that the acceleration due to gravity is 32 feet per second per second?"

"If I think a long time back to my physics classes, that does sound correct, although that per second per second concept always confused me."

"It means that when the ball falls it will be going 32 feet per second faster at the end of each second. So, when it hangs motionless on the ceiling it is going zero feet per second, and one second later it will be going 32 feet per second. If we add those two together—zero plus 32, and average the number, we get 16 feet. Which, of course, is the height of the train car."

I looked at him in confusion. "If you say so."

"I do say so. The ball will drop 16 feet in one second. So if you are sitting at the siding looking through the wall of the train car and we turn off the magnet it will take exactly one second for the ball to drop the sixteen feet to the floor of the car directly below its suspension point."

"All right. I understand what you're saying."

Cassius smiled at me. "Good, good. Now let's change one little thing. Let's start the train car moving. In fact let's back the train down the track and start it moving at 60 miles per hour. At that speed the train will move 88 feet in one second." He looked at my face. "I can do the mathematics for you, if you'd like."

"No, no. I'm sure you're right."

"Oh, I am. Now let's drop the ball from the ceiling again when the car is 88 feet away from your spot at the siding. Remember the train is moving 60 miles per hour so it will take it exactly one second to pass you. Where will the ball land?"

I thought about the problem for a moment. "I'm not sure."

"If you were in the train car you would see it land on the floor exactly where it did when the train was standing still. Why? Because the ball is travelling at the same speed as the train."

"I think I understand." I tried to visualize the scene he had described.

"Trust me, it will. But how far will the ball really have traveled?"

"Sixteen feet?"

"Vertically sixteen feet, but remember the train has moved forward 88 feet while the ball was dropping." He raised his right hand up and drew a diagonal line down toward his left knee. "In other words the ball has traveled forward 88 feet while it fell 16 feet to the floor. If you were sitting at the siding, watching the ball through the glass wall of the train car, you would see the ball move diagonally. The diagonal line it traversed is just over 89 feet long."

"I think I understand."

"Trust me, Pythagoras wasn't wrong. But if the ball has traveled so much further I pose the next question—how long did it take for the ball to reach the floor?"

I wrinkled my forehead. "I'm not sure."

"If you were on the train, it would take one second!" He smiled at my puzzlement. "In other words, the faster the train goes, the further the ball travels, but it will still take exactly one second. Now, if you were stationary at the crossing and had a very, very accurate clock, it would take a little longer than a second."

"How can that be? It just doesn't make sense."

Cassius smiled. "Because time changes the faster we travel. It goes slower. Einstein tried to explain it. Astronauts had to make corrections to their clocks to account for it."

"But I thought the one thing that couldn't change was time."

Cassius shook his head. "It does seem strange doesn't it? But I've wandered on too long. The bottom line is that if that train were traveling the speed of light, time would stand still. I know it's hard to understand, but, trust me, it's true."

"Still," I said, "what does that have to do with no past or future?"

"God is a God of light. He travels at that speed, so time stands still. Remember what Matthew said, 'thy whole body shall be full of light?'"

"That is so hard to comprehend," I said shaking my head.

"How else do you think Moses and Nephi saw the end from the beginning? Everything co-exists in the time we call now."

"But that means that if everything has already

happened, I had no control over what happened with my life. This sounds like pre-destination to me."

"Well, you might think so," said Cassius. "There are many here who have taken great comfort in that thought. Of course, it isn't, but it would take a considerable amount of time to explain." He paused a moment, "And some have felt great pain, as well." He stood up and extended his hand. "I hope you find our kingdom to your liking. I hate to abandon you, but I have a fairly full schedule." He led me to the door, which opened as we approached.

Chapter 3

The street had cleared of most of the people and I was able to look down one of the wide avenues unimpeded. It was clear that this was a glorious city. I had never seen anything like it in the extensive travels I had taken throughout my life. I was still wrestling with the idea Cassius had explained as I wandered down the seamless pavement. Beautiful buildings surrounded me on all sides. Some seemed to be constructed of a fine-grained marble that fairly glowed within an interior radiance, others of a polished metallic material that refracted the light into rainbow hues including a color I had never before seen. I touched the surface of one building and felt its warmth radiate into me. Hours passed as I walked among these impressive edifices, awestruck by the beauty and size of the city. At length I felt hungry—the sandwich Cassius had supplied was a distant memory. I looked for somewhere to get something to eat, but there were no signs attached to any of the buildings. Finally, I approached a woman who was standing in the doorway of one of the marble monuments.

"Excuse me, I'm new here. Is there any place I could get a meal?"

She smiled at me. "Of course, just follow me," she said as she beckoned with her hand.

The door of the building slid open with a hiss and I

followed her into the lobby. She led me under the beautifully decorated dome and through a veritable forest of greenery to a small, secluded room. The walls were lined with small booths. The seats were upholstered in a shimmering ivory fabric that immediately conformed to my body as I seated myself.

"I hope this will do," the woman said with a smile.

"I'm sure it will be fine." I looked around the room. It was decorated in the same shiny metallic surface I had seen on so many of the buildings. The lighting was subdued, but a single white spotlight shined on the wall opposite our booth and sent a spectrum of color flashing across the ceiling. There were no other customers; in fact, no one else was visible. "I'm not sure how to order—is there a menu?"

She slid into the seat across from me. "You really are new, aren't you? Do you mind if I sit here and help you?"

"Not at all," I said, smiling. I studied her face. It was difficult to determine her age, but she had an alluring quality about her. "Please show me what to do."

"What would you like to eat?"

"Nothing fancy. Maybe a hamburger?"

"I'm sorry, that's not on the menu."

"What would you suggest?" I asked.

"Maybe it would be easier if I ordered for you. If you don't mind?"

"Please," I said.

She lifted her hand from the table top and placed it against the wall. Immediately the surface shimmered from opaque to transparent and, I suppose, showed a menu. I did not recognize the language. She slid her finger down the list and tapped it twice. She removed her hand from the wall and it restored itself to opacity once again.

"I hope this will be satisfactory," she said with a smile as a section of the wall opposite our booth slid open and a man walked quickly to our table and placed a tray on it.

"Please enjoy," he said with a slight bow as he turned and left us.

My companion lifted the cover on the tray and revealed two plates with steaming food on them. I lifted them while she slid the tray off the table and deposited it on a shelf behind her seat. Immediately the tray disappeared from view. I looked for silverware, and finding none, said, "Looks like he forgot to bring utensils."

The woman tapped the wall where it joined our table and a small opening appeared. She reached in and removed two sets of silverware wrapped tightly in linen napkins. "These should suffice," she said with a simple smile.

"Thank you," I said. "You've been most kind. I suppose I should introduce myself. My name is Mark."

"It has been my pleasure, Mark. They call me Cleo." She unfolded the napkin, picked up a shining silver fork, and took a dainty bite of food.

The food was delicious. "What do they call this?" I asked, pointing at my plate with my fork.

"Number eight," she replied.

"But doesn't it have a name?" I asked.

Cleo shrugged her shoulders. "Not that I know. It's just number eight." She looked past me at the wall behind me.

"I'd give anything for a drink of that," she said as she ran her tongue over her upper lip.

I turned and looked over my shoulder. There were three shelves filled with bottles of liquor that ran the full width of the room. Each bottle had a festive label attached to it.

"Please don't let me stop you," I said.

She took her eyes off the bottles and looked me in the face. The smile on her face was one of sadness. "You're not stopping me. They're just there for show. They don't have anything in them."

"I don't understand."

"They're just there to remind us of past decisions and habits."

"Why not remove them?"

"I'm afraid that can't be done. They are there to remind us," she repeated with sorrow in her voice. "I'd better go."

I could see the anguish in her face. "Must you?"

She nodded her head. "It's very painful sitting here with that constant reminder."

"Change places with me," I suggested.

She laughed a hollow laugh. "You don't understand, do you?" She slid out of her seat and changed places with me. I looked at the wall behind her and the bottles had disappeared, but when I looked over my shoulder they had reappeared behind me.

"They're always there," she indicated in a throaty whisper. "I really must go."

She slid out of the booth and started toward the exit. I hurried to catch her. "Thank you for your help."

"Don't mention it." She slipped through the portal and back onto the street. I turned back to the table we had occupied to find the dishes had been cleared. The bottles were nowhere to be seen.

Chapter 4

As I left the restaurant I noticed more congestion on the sidewalk. I felt myself pushed along with the throng to a round-a-bout where eight roads converged. I made my way to the small park in the center of the circle and found a sign post identifying where each of the streets led. The road I had just walked down led to Paulstown, and going around the circle were roads leading to Appolonia, Petersburg, Johnstown, Mosheville, Ellyahtown, Esaiasburg, and Hanokhfield. I sat down on one of three benches arranged in a triangle in the middle of the park and contemplated the beauty of this wonderful place. Barely a minute passed before a tall man pushed his way through the crowd and stood next to my bench.

"May I sit with you?" he asked.

"Of course," I said, sliding to one end of the bench.

"Thank you." He lowered himself gently beside me. "It is a wondrous kingdom, is it not?" he asked, almost to himself.

"It is," I agreed.

"I wonder how the vote went?" he mused.

"I don't know," I stammered.

The man shifted his robe higher on his shoulder. "Inevitable," he said.

"I don't understand."

"They're coming, whether we want to embrace them or not."

"Oh." I waited for a response and when none came, I said, "What impact will that bring?"

The man rubbed his chin thoughtfully, "Well the sifting process has gone on. Many would say those who are coming now are the bottom of the barrel, so to speak. But as to an impact? Not much, except the incessant grab for power." He turned his head and looked me straight in the eye, "I suppose it all comes down to that—power."

"Does it bother you?"

He shrugged his shoulders. "Not really. Of course each of us thinks he is right and the others are wrong, so the debates will continue." He continued to gaze at my face. "You're new here, aren't you?"

I nodded my head. "And have you decided who you'll follow? Where you'll live?"

"I don't think I'm staying," I replied. "I'm just visiting."

He raised an eyebrow, "Really? How odd." He gestured with his hands, "but why would you want to leave? Don't you think this is truly glorious?"

"It is. More wonderful than anything I've ever seen."

"Then why leave?"

"I'm not sure," I replied.

He smiled at me, "You're not one of those social climbers, are you?"

"Oh, no," I said shaking my head. "Not at all."

"You haven't been swayed by William's words?"

I looked at him with confusion, "William?"

"Oh, I see, you haven't met him yet. Well, you will. He

tells a wonderful story, but I'd suggest you stay away from him. His ways are truly strange."

"You sound as if you are dissatisfied yourself."

"Not really," he replied. "It's just that sometimes it gets wearisome with all of the wrangling that goes on," he sighed.

"When I leave why don't you come with me?"

He massaged his temples with his fingertips. "It would be more miserable to dwell in a kingdom with those who are more just and holy and be conscious of your own shortcomings than to have continued to dwell with the damned souls of hell," he said, almost under his breath. "No, I think I'm more comfortable here." He stood slowly up and looked at me. Although he smiled, I sensed a deep regret hiding behind his eyes. Without another word he nodded his head in my direction and re-entered the crowd that milled around the round-about.

I sat contemplating his words, realizing I had not even learned his name, when another man freed himself from the crowd and sat down next to me on the bench.

"Glorious day, isn't it?" he said while he flashed a smile in my direction.

I nodded my head, "Yes, it is."

"I'm William," he said extending his hand.

"They call me Mark," I replied.

"And you're new here, aren't you?"

"Yes. I'm not sure why everyone can tell that, but I'm just visiting."

William slid closer to me on the bench. "Have you decided where you're going to settle down? I can help you get the biggest palace you're entitled to." He pointed down the street toward Appolonia. "There are some wonderful properties available in a very enviable neighborhood. If you know what I mean." He bumped my shoulder with his. "All of the comforts are close at hand."

"I don't believe I'm staying," I replied.

"Of course you're staying, or you wouldn't be here. You've paid the final farthing, so to speak, haven't you? You must have or you wouldn't have gotten out of prison and come here." He slid his arm around my shoulders and gave me a hug. "And I'd be delighted to help you get everything you've earned." He smiled again. "Might I ask your occupation? I was a lawyer and a politician and thankfully both are still needed, unlike some professions."

"I'm just a teacher," I replied.

He flashed an even bigger smile. "Never say just a teacher. They are most highly respected and esteemed." He hugged me again. "And desperately needed, I might add. With those millions of souls still needing to be taught, you'll be very busy. Thankfully you're not a doctor or a wig maker, they're really in need of job retraining. Now, how about my offer? Why don't you let me take you to Appolonia and get you moved in?"

I stood up and turned to William. "I do appreciate your offer, but as I said, I'm not staying. Thank you anyway." I started to leave when William sprang to his feet and grabbed my arm.

"I don't think you understand the whole situation," he said. "There will be many who will try to lead you astray. Please let me help you."

I was becoming slightly uncomfortable with his insistence. "If there are so many who are trying to lead us astray, perhaps you could explain to me why I should trust you?"

His countenance darkened slightly, and he leaned toward me conspiratorially. "The others claim to know the truth, but I am the only one who has gone back to the old, true ways. They argue about matters that truly do not matter. I am the only one who knows what 'is' is."

I looked confused. "I'm not sure I understand what you mean."

"Just trust me," he plead. "Our community is a wonderful place to live. We have everything that one could desire. Well, nearly everything. I'd give anything for a good cigar. There are restrictions to keep the riff-raff out." He patted his chest with the palm of his hand.

I looked past William at the milling crowd and asked, "What kinds of restrictions?"

"I'm not at liberty to explain unless you agree to ally yourself with us."

I shook my head slightly, "Are children allowed?"

"Children? No, of course not, there are no children here."

I inspected the milling crowd, "None?"

William shook his head, "I don't mean to be abrupt, but I need to have your decision. It's not that I don't like you, you understand, but there are so many others that I need to contact."

"I really am just visiting," I replied.

He shrugged his shoulders. "I feel sorry for you," he said. "You sound as if you don't know what you want." Without any further indication, he stepped back into the crowd.

Chapter 5

I chose a direction opposite the one I had seen William take and joined the crowd. We flowed down the avenue toward Mosheville and as we continued past the skyscrapers the vista opened ahead to broad manicured lawns and gardens of flowers that perfumed the air. I stepped to the edge of the milling crowd and tried to get my bearings. The grass cushioned my feet and felt comforting to my touch.

"Lost?" I felt a hand on my shoulder.

"Sort of—well, not really," I replied as I turned to see who was speaking. A tall, white-haired man stood beside me. "I'm just visiting," I explained before he suggested that I was new.

He raised an eyebrow. "Oh? That's peculiar." He rubbed his clean-shaven chin with his hand. "And just where did you come from?"

"A small town—not one you'd have heard of."

"That small?" he said with a smile.

"My great-grandfather founded it. Unlike most of my cousins, I stayed around. I taught school for nearly forty years," I rambled on.

"And where are you going? If I might ask?"

"I'm not sure of that either. I have a guide who has been showing me—"

"Oh? Where is he?"

"Well, not really showing me," I mumbled, "just kind of dropping me off at the gate, so to speak."

"Ah! Well, did you enjoy teaching?"

I chewed on my lower lip, "Yes, yes I did." I finally stammered.

"Did you find it rewarding?"

"I suppose. There were always a few students I didn't seem to reach, but for the most part I think I did some good."

"You're not alone."

"What?"

"Even though all of these souls recognize the Master, not all of them follow him. Do you understand what I'm saying?"

I furrowed my brow, "Not really."

The tall man patted my arm. "What I'm saying is that quite a number of his students didn't pay attention either."

"Oh! Well, might I inquire as to what you're doing?"

He smiled at me, "I suppose you could say I'm involved in a reclamation project." He barely suppressed a low chuckle. "May I walk with you?" He gestured down the pathway with his hand.

"I suppose," I replied.

We re-entered the flow of people streaming down the pathway until my companion pointed to a bench situated beneath a tree that burst with blossoms. "Why don't we sit for a moment?" He pointed at the bench and we sat down. The perfume from the blossoms surrounded and soothed us.

"Thank you for just resting a minute," I said. "Everyone seems so rushed—so busy."

"There's a lot of work to do," my companion replied with a gentle smile. "It is a busy place." He leaned back and inhaled deeply. "Have you met many of the residents?"

"A few. They seem like interesting people. They're quite intense."

"That's a good description—intense. Each group is convinced that it is right and the others are wrong. It leads to quite a bit of controversy and proselytizing. It would be humorous if it weren't so serious."

We sat silently for a few moments watching the crowd flow by. "May I ask which of the groups you have joined?"

He ran his hands through his hair, "Oh, none of them. I'm a messenger from another kingdom."

"Oh?"

"We visit and try to teach, but old habits die hard." He smiled grimly. "But, of course, we'll never quit trying." He rose softly to his feet. "May I give you some advice?"

"Of course."

"Listen to the Guide."

"That's all?"

He nodded. "It is enough." With a gentle wave of his hand he left me and joined the crowd.

I looked back toward the city and decided it was time to take my leave. Although it seemed as if I had walked a long way into the countryside, I was able to return to the city gates in but a few minutes. The beauty of the kingdom beckoned to me but, gathering my resolve, I walked out of the city gate and said quietly, "I'm ready to go." Almost immediately I saw the point of light in the distance begin to move toward me and within a few moments the Guide stood at my side.

"A beautiful kingdom, isn't it?"

"Yes," I replied, "a wonderful place." I turned toward Him. "Why did I feel uncomfortable?"

He smiled gently at me. "Because you didn't belong." He indicated the path with His hand. "Shall we?"

Chapter 6

We climbed the path in silence for several minutes and then I said, "They seem like good people."

The Guide smiled, "There are some very good people among them."

"I spoke to several of them. They seemed genuine in their beliefs."

The Guide nodded His head. "Do you understand what commitment means?"

"I think so."

"It is quite easy to profess something with your lips, but much more difficult to truly commit yourself to a way of life." He paused as we walked further along the path. "Their hearts really aren't in it," He said with sadness in His voice.

I could see a glow in the distance and as we walked closer to it the brightness increased until we stood at the gates of a city. The walls stretched upward until they seemed to touch the clouds. The Guide led me to the tall, opulent, silver-clad doors that opened noiselessly at our approach. Two men stood inside the doors and bowed slightly as we approached. The Guide smiled at them.

"I'll be here," He said, inclining His head toward a snow-white, glittering building just inside the doors, "when you're ready to go."

He walked toward a recessed doorway that opened to

admit Him as He approached. I stood uncertainly and looked into the city. The streets seemed paved with silver. It was not nearly as crowded as the previous kingdom, but still a good number of souls were moving purposely through the town square. One of the men who had greeted us moved to my side.

"May I be of help?"

"Yes, I mean, I suppose so. I'm not really sure why I'm here."

He nodded his head slightly and smiled at me. "Perhaps I might suggest you visit the Hall of Fame." He gestured with his hand toward a towering, domed building on the right side of the square. "I think many of your questions might be answered there."

I bowed slightly in return. "Thank you. I'll take your suggestion." I turned and started to walk toward the building when I spotted a familiar figure walking down the street. "Brother Johnson," I called out.

The man turned and looked at me. His forehead wrinkled. "Who is it that calls my old name?"

I walked quickly to him and extended my hand. "Brother Johnson, don't you remember me?"

He squinted his eyes and looked at my face. Suddenly a flood of recognition washed over him. "You're Mark, aren't you?"

"Yes. You were my home teacher, Brother Johnson."

A cloud crossed his face. "Not a very good one, I'm afraid."

"Why do you say that?"

"I wasn't very faithful."

"You were busy, very busy as I remember, but you came when time permitted."

"Usually on the last day of the month," he said uncomfortably.

"Not always," I replied, "sometimes it was earlier."

He smiled a wan smile. "I appreciate your kindness, but I've stopped making excuses for myself." His eyes searched my face. "Can you forgive me for not giving you the service you deserved?"

"Of course," I said patting him on the shoulder. "I'm just delighted to see you. It's always wonderful to see someone you know."

"Yes, yes it is. What brings you here?" he asked.

"I'm just visiting. I'm really not sure why—I've been a couple of other places and now I'm here. I just barely arrived."

"Well, I wish I had time to show you around. But I have an assignment I'm trying to finish and I'm late as usual." He shrugged his shoulders.

"I understand," I replied. "I was just going into the Hall of Fame."

He turned to go. "Well, have a good visit. It was good—somewhat painful—but good to see you again." He hurried off down the street and then over his shoulder called out, "There are several others here you'll recognize." He took several quick steps then over his shoulder asked, "Will you be here later to hear the debate?"

"I don't know. I'm really not sure how long I'll be here. Who is debating?"

"George and Phillip," he replied. "It will be a spirited debate, I'm sure."

"And what will they be debating?"

"Foreordination versus predestination. I hope to see

you there." He continued to walk briskly down the street.

I waved good-bye and turned toward the Hall of Fame. A young woman stood at the door and greeted me as I approached.

"Welcome, friend," she said with a smile.

"Thank you," I replied.

The door opened as I approached and I entered a circular room whose floors were paved with embossed silver squares and whose walls were made of curiously carved marble. In the center of the hall was a raised platform with a doughnut-shaped desk perhaps thirty feet in diameter. Within the doughnut about two dozen people sat at the desk with small translucent screens in front of them from which they were apparently reading. I watched curiously as one of the men touched the screen with a stylus and a path of light followed its point across the surface. I turned and looked at the room. The walls had carved niches with silver plaques bracketing them. I summoned my courage and approached the raised desk.

One of the men working there stood as I approached and inclined his head. "May I help you?"

"I'm visiting," I replied. "Is there anything I should know—any rule—about looking at your collection?"

"You haven't been here before, have you? Well, feel free to look at any of our displays. If you place your hand on the plaque to the right of the display you'll hear the person's voice. If you place your hand on the plaque to the left of the display you'll be able to view some of the person's accomplishments." He smiled. "Anything else I can help you with?"

"Not really," I began to turn, "well, perhaps you could answer one question?"

"I'll try."

"Who is here? I mean who's being honored?"

"It changes," he replied with a slight smile. "Whomever you honored will likely be here."

"I don't understand."

"Perhaps it will be clearer to you as you take a little tour of our facility." He pointed toward the niche closest to the doorway through which I had entered. "That would be a good place to start."

"Thank you." I stepped down from the dais and walked toward the first niche, which, like all the others, appeared to be an empty, lighted nook about three feet high and a foot wide with a curved back that extended eight or so inches into the wall. The two silver panels on each side of it merely had the faint imprint of a hand. Slowly I extended my right hand and placed it within the outline on the silver panel. Within the niche the lights dimmed and a three-dimensional image of a man's head appeared. He looked vaguely familiar, but I could not place him precisely. As I looked at the man his eyes slowly opened and he began to speak.

"Welcome, Mark. Perhaps you do not remember me. I served you in the senate." He paused.

Suddenly I remembered the man. Many years before I had helped him work on his campaign and he had won the election. He had been quite elderly, as I recalled, and the man who spoke to me now was in the prime of life.

"I remember," I said.

The visage smiled. "Good." He looked straight into my eyes, "What brings you here?"

"I'm visiting," I replied. "Might I ask you the same

question? And, is this all there is of you?" I extended my hand toward the bust I saw before me.

He chuckled, "Oh, no. This is my representation in the Hall of Fame. I'm busy working, as we all are. I'm honored that you summoned me here."

"I don't understand."

"The Hall of Fame is very specific, Mark. Those of this kingdom whom you honored in life are here to greet you."

"I think I understand, although I don't see how it all works." I stood silently before him for a moment. "I certainly did hold you in the highest regard," I finally said. "What specifically has brought you to this place?"

For just a brief moment it seemed that the man's gaze clouded and his cheeks sagged and then he spoke. "As you probably remember, I was so sure those liberals were going to bring down the country. I knew the end was in sight and that we were in for some rough times. Lucifer is so clever, I thought the enemy was there in that liberal camp. I had no idea that the extremists in either direction become part of the problem."

"I'm not sure what you mean," I interjected.

"We were so convinced we were right and all the others were wrong. They were trying to soften the laws and we were trying to hold strictly to them. We were the inter-preters of the Founding Fathers' wishes and desires. And so we became deluded and believed that the end justified the means."

I nodded my head. "You always seemed to stand for what was right."

He blinked his eyes rapidly. "I thought I was right. I was convinced of a conspiracy against truth and so I used any means to protect my position. Any means!"

The man's face in front of me displayed a mix of passion and dismay.

"I'm still not sure what you mean."

Again his cheeks sagged and his gaze dropped to the floor before me. "We misrepresented some facts. No, let me be honest, we kept back some of the information. We felt it was necessary to reach our goals. Such noble goals."

The face began to fade. His eyes shut and like a wisp of vapor the visage before me shimmered and disappeared. I stood pondering what he had said, then I extended my left hand and placed it on the silver plaque on the opposite side of the niche. Immediately the empty niche was filled with a three-dimensional image of a room. The senator sat at a table while others milled around him. The conversation rumbled and I found it hard to focus on any of it. The senator raised a gavel and rapped it on the table. Quickly the conversations ended and he called the meeting to order. A woman I did not recognize walked to his side and whispered something in his ear. A flash of fear crossed his face and he began to speak earnestly. I could not follow the conversation—obviously I was witnessing something that had been going on for some time and I entered near the end of the deliberations. I placed my hand on the plaque again and the scene changed.

I stood with the senator on the brow of a low hill. The wind toyed with his silver hair as he looked at the development going on below. Dozens of homes were under construction. Behind him was a sign designating the development as a planned, secure community. I tapped the plaque again.

We were in a church listening to a sermon. The speaker was talking about loving our fellow man and the senator was taking notes on a yellow pad. I looked over his shoulder and noticed that what he was writing bore no resemblance to the speaker's sermon. I removed my hand from the plaque and the niche became empty again. Confused, I placed my right hand on the first plaque I had touched and watched as the senator's bust appeared again. Slowly his eyes opened.

"Well, Mark, thank you for visiting."

"Thank you," I replied. "I just witnessed some scenes from your past."

"Ah, yes."

"But I'm not sure I understand them."

"What did you see?" he asked.

"You were in a meeting of some sort with a gavel in your hand."

The smile broadened on his face. "That was when we passed the child protection bill," he said. "Of all the legislation I sponsored, it had the most far-reaching effects. Pride is a sin, but I must say I'm proud of what that accomplished. Even if we had to ignore some of the evidence."

"I can understand that," I said returning his smile.

"What else did you see?" he queried.

"I saw you standing on a hilltop surveying a community and I saw you in church taking notes."

"The planned and gated development where we lived," he said. "A safe haven amidst the turmoil of the world. A place where those of us who thought alike could live in peace."

"And were you happy there?" I asked.

"I suppose," he replied thoughtfully. "At least we were comfortable."

"And the scene in church?" I queried.

He sighed. "Sometimes my mind was so full of my other responsibilities I refused to listen to those things that were really important." He blinked, "I suppose I began to believe I was above all that sermonizing. I was wrong. I hope you understand."

"Thank you," I said thoughtfully. "You've given me much to think about."

"May I give you some advice?"

"Certainly."

"I must call on more of my own experiences. I hope you will forgive me for that." He looked into my eyes and I nodded. "I listened a great deal to the philosophies of men and I thought I lived a good life, but only after I arrived here did I gain a testimony of my Savior. Don't make the same mistake I made." His eyes shut and he began to fade again.

"It may be too late," I replied as he dissolved into nothingness.

I turned on the silver floor and moved to the next niche. Before I placed my hand on the plaque I looked over my shoulder at the people working inside the doughnut. They appeared completely oblivious to my presence. With some trepidation I placed my hand against the cool silver plate.

Chapter 7

A vaguely familiar face began to form in the niche, a face I had not seen in over fifty years. I struggled to put a name with the image that formed before me. Slowly his eyes opened and he looked at me. His eyes were dark, chocolate pools. I saw the recognition flood through them.

"Elder," he said enthusiastically.

Memories flooded my mind. "Juan?" I asked tentatively.

"Yes! It is so good to see you again."

I remembered back to a beautiful home in Barcelona where I had first met Juan. My companion and I had considered him a golden contact. He was a physician of some renown and he and his family lived in an estate on the edge of the city. I remembered sitting in the shade of flowering trees in the atrium of their home listening to the soothing sounds of water cascading down the multi-tiered fountain that graced the center of the patio.

"My friend," he said, "I thought I would never see you again. Where is Elder Walker?"

"I'm not sure where he is, Juan. When we were transferred we each ended up with another companion." My mind flashed back to experiences of over half a century before. "And shortly after that I was released to return home. Elder Walker served nearly another year before his release. We kind of lost track of each other over the intervening years."

"I understand," the visage said. "It is easy to lose track of that which is important."

I gazed deeply into his eyes. "You were such a good man with such a wonderful family."

"You are too kind." He lowered his eyes. "We should have listened to you. I—we knew what you were teaching was true, but it was so hard to turn our backs on our family. It would have killed my father if I had abandoned the customs he embraced."

"I understand."

"But does it not say, 'a man should leave his father and mother?'"

"It does. But I still understand how difficult that would be."

"Of course that was not all. Many of my patients heard of my interest in this new religion and they were skeptical. I was afraid of losing them—of losing the income." He stopped for a moment, "But these are just excuses—aren't they. Excuses to try to justify my actions." His eyes shut for a moment and when they reopened I could see the sadness in them. "You tried so hard to help me see and now that I'm here I know you were right."

"We loved you so much," I said softly.

"And you honored us with so much of your time," he replied as he began to fade. "Thank you for letting me see you again." His voice trailed off as the image disappeared.

I placed my left hand on the other plaque and immediately I saw Juan walking through a thatched-roofed village to a mud-floored hut where he began giving medical attention to an endless stream of the poor, and I knew why he was honored. I turned back to the raised dais and climbed the step until I stood in front of one of the translucent screens. A tall, angelic woman smiled at me.

"May I help you?" she said.

"I just wanted to thank you for the opportunity of visiting."

"You've only looked at two of our—your—honorees," she said. "Feel free to take as much time as you'd like."

"I think I've seen enough."

"Most of our visitors feel the same way," she said smiling. "It is a time filled with both joy and sadness for most of them."

"Yes," I simply replied, nodding my head. I looked at the screen that stood between us. "Might I ask what you are doing?"

"It might be a little difficult to explain," she said, "but I'll try. We are erasing events."

"Erasing?"

"That they be remembered no more," she said with an enigmatic smile. "Is there anything else I can help you with?" She extended the stylus in her hand and drew it across the screen leaving a streak of light.

"These people," I indicated with a sweep of my hand toward the niches, "seem like very good people. They accomplished a great deal of good in their lives."

"A great deal," she nodded in agreement.

"What brings them here?"

"You did," she said simply.

"I'm beginning to understand that, but, collectively, what brought them here, to this kingdom?"

"Most of them were blinded by something that kept them from completely embracing the Master. It might have been fame or fortune. It might have been the craftiness of other men. Some just didn't have the opportunity to hear and accept the law."

"But that hardly seems fair," I interjected.

"Ah—but they would not have accepted it had they heard it." The stylus zipped across the screen leaving another streak of light. "There are many here who were like Thomas of old, who could not believe on the word and deeds of others, but required a first-hand experience to come to an understanding of what they needed to know and accept. But perhaps that is hard for you to understand?"

"Perhaps. It always seemed so clear to me."

The stylus raced across the screen. "I know, Mark." She smiled a knowing smile. "I hope you enjoy your stay."

"How did you know my name?"

"Oh, you are quite well known," she replied turning her attention back to the screen.

I stepped down from the dais and walked toward the doorway through which I had entered. It opened quietly and I stepped through the doorway into the street. The same young woman who had greeted me bowed slightly and said, "Thank you for coming. Please feel free to return any time. Peace be with you."

"Thank you," I replied and stepped onto the silver-paved pavement.

Chapter 8

The glistening streets stretched like a fan from the Hall of Fame and I was able to look down each one from my focal point. I could see people moving busily down the streets. Each seemed to be surrounded with a soft glow that I had not noticed before. I looked back at the building where my Guide had entered and then decided to spend more time in this wondrous realm. Deliberately I chose the first street on my left and started walking down the spotless path. Glistening buildings rose on either side forming a marble canyon with a silver floor and an azure-crowned ceiling. A small crowd of souls was gathered in the intersection and, as I approached, their circle opened up, as if on command, and I was included in the group.

"Have you received your assignment yet?" a tall, silver-haired man asked.

"Not yet. I expect to hear very soon," a shorter gentleman with piercing blue eyes replied.

The others in the circle nodded their heads.

"And you, Lucius?"

The tall man nodded his head. "I have come to say good-bye."

A murmur passed among them. "You will do well. You always have," the blue-eyed man replied.

"I hope so. They say the work is hard there." He looked directly into my eyes. "Do I know you? You seem somewhat familiar, but I don't remember seeing you before."

I nodded my head, "I arrived a short time ago. I think I'm just visiting."

"Oh?" The tall man continued to stare into my face.

"Might I ask where you are going?"

"Of course," he extended his hands and took mine in his. "I'm leaving on a mission to the lower kingdom, to preach and teach and hope to bring some of them into a realization of the truth."

"I have been there," I said simply.

An exclamation of surprise went up collectively from the group.

"You will have your work cut out for you," I said simply

"I know that," he said softly.

"And if you succeed, will you bring them back with you?" I asked.

He dropped my hands and shook his head slowly. "No, but I can help them advance within their kingdom. As you probably noticed, there are great differences within that kingdom and we would hope for the best for everyone who lives there."

"Well, I wish you the best of luck," I said, turning to go.

"Thank you," he replied. "I intend to do all I can." He shook hands with each of the others and walked past me toward the gate of the city.

"He will do well," one of the others said as the group dissipated and walked away in several directions. Only the short, blue-eyed man remained.

"You say you are just visiting?" he asked.

I nodded my head.

"I know the kingdom well, would you like me to guide you?"

"That would be most kind."

"Where would you like to go?" he asked.

"I don't know," I replied frankly. "I'm not familiar at all with what is here."

"Then permit me," he said, taking my arm. "If I am not mistaken, your name is Mark. They call me Benedict."

We started to walk slowly down the street and he told me of the labors going on in each of the buildings we passed. At length we stopped in front of an edifice with intricately carved symbols in its front.

"This is where I work," Benedict said with reverence. "Would you like to see my office?"

"With pleasure," I replied.

We walked through an open archway into the building. Benedict nodded to two people who sat at glass-topped pedestals on either side of the arch. They returned his greeting with small bows. We crossed the lobby and stepped into a crystal-fronted chamber that whisked us upward rapidly. When the chamber opened we stepped into an office that was paneled in an iridescent material that reflected and refracted rainbow hues across the floor. A larger glass-topped pedestal seemed to float above the floor in the center of the room. A comfortable chair, uphol-stered in gleaming white fabric, sat behind it.

"My humble office," Benedict said with a smile. He indicated a snow-white couch that rested against one wall. "Please have a seat."

"Thank you," I said taking a seat. Benedict sat on the other end of the couch. "May I ask what you do here?"

"Of course. I'm in charge of agriculture for the third quadrant," he said simply. "Would you like to see the farms?"

I began to push myself to my feet. "Yes," I said simply.

"Oh, we don't have to leave," he said simply and pointed his hand toward the iridescent wall behind the desk. Immediately, as if a curtain were being raised, a picture appeared on the wall. An extensive orchard extended to the horizon.

"What a beautiful orchard," I exclaimed. "And what a remarkable picture."

"Thank you. We should begin harvesting the fruit at any moment."

As if at that command I watched a group of people walk amongst the trees and begin pulling fruit from their branches. We watched as baskets seemed to float beside them. A second group of workers retrieved the containers as they were filled and replaced them with empty ones.

"It seems to be a very orderly operation," I said admiringly.

"Yes, it is," Benedict said with just a touch of pride in his voice. "We supply a bountiful harvest for the people. No one goes hungry."

"That is admirable," I replied. "I've seen so much hunger—famine really—in my life."

Benedict looked at me with a bit of a frown. "But it did not have to be, you know. There was always enough, if we had been able to share. But then that has always been the problem, hasn't it—sharing?" He extended his hand toward the wall and the picture vanished.

We sat in comfortable silence for a few minutes and then I asked, "Could you answer something for me?"

"Of course."

"Your friend, Lucius, seemed both excited and

reluctant to leave this kingdom on his mission."

"Yes, I suppose that is true."

"And you all seemed to expect to do the same."

"Yes. We're all involved in teaching, when the call comes. It is the least we can do after the Savior sent his emissaries to us when we languished in prison." Tears filled his eyes. "It is the least we can do." We lapsed back into silence until another man entered the room. He was large in stature and strode purposely across the floor.

"Excuse me," he said. "I didn't know we had a guest." His eyebrows rose as he looked at me. Then he walked toward me and extended his hand. "My name is Luther," he said with a smile.

Benedict rose quickly from his end of the couch and said, "Excuse me for not introducing you. This is Mark."

"I'm pleased to meet you," I replied as I struggled to my feet.

"Oh, no, it is my pleasure," he replied. He smiled a broad smile as he turned to my host. "Benedict, when you are through, Gregor and I have something to show you."

"Don't let me stop you," I said quickly. "I've taken too much of your time already."

"Nonsense," Benedict replied. He focused his attention on Luther. "I'll be there shortly."

"It has been wonderful to meet you," Luther said as he turned to go. "Welcome to our humble home." He retreated through the archway.

"Quite a remarkable fellow," Benedict said. "Almost single-handedly kept the Irish from starving."

My forehead wrinkled, "Oh?"

"Something to do with blight-resistant potatoes, I believe."

"I'd like to hear that story, sometime," I replied. "He seems excited about what he has to show you."

"He knew a great deal in his former life, and whatever intelligence he attained there has been amplified. He has much the advantage over me in this world."

"I'm beginning to understand," I said.

"Mark, all truth is independent, as is all intelligence, and that gives meaning to our existence." He looked longingly toward the archway where Luther had left.

"You have been most kind," I said, extending my hand. "But let me get on with your labors."

"Know you are welcome any time, Mark," he said, taking my hand in his as he gently guided me through the archway and back onto the street.

"Thank you for your time," I replied.

Benedict nodded his head, turned, and walked back through the arch. I watched him go until he turned and waved to me. I returned the wave and then walked back down the street toward the Hall of Fame.

Chapter 9

I reached the junction of the streets and paused to ponder on what I'd learned when the woman who stood sentinel at the Hall of Fame beckoned to me. I walked to where she stood.

"I'm glad you have not left," she said with a warm smile. "There is someone who wanted to meet you."

I raised my eyebrows. "Really?"

She nodded her head. "If you'll stay here, I'll go get him." She turned with a swish of her robes and walked quickly into the Hall of Fame. It seemed but a brief moment before she reappeared with a strapping young man at her side.

"This is David," she said simply. "He wanted to thank you."

"So you are Mark," he said with a gleaming smile as he grasped my hand in his. "I owe much to you."

"I'm sorry," I said, puzzled. "Do I know you?"

He laughed a low, throaty laugh. "Ah, you have forgotten."

"You have me at your mercy," I replied.

"But then you went so often how could I expect you to remember my poor name." He continued to hold my hand in his and he led me to a low marble bench surrounded by flowering shrubs. "Please, have a seat."

I withdrew my hand and sat on one end of the bench.

"Please tell me what I have forgotten," I queried the young man who sat on the other end of the marble seat.

"You did my work for me," he said patting his chest with his right hand.

"Your work?"

"In the temple," he replied. "Although, I must admit, I did not fully take advantage of the opportunity you extended." He flashed his smile at me again. "But perhaps I should explain."

"Yes," I said, "please do."

He leaned back against the shrubbery and brought both hands together in front of him palms up. "I had been schooled in the noble eightfold path of enlightenment. I strove with all my heart to live those noble attributes and become a true believer and practitioner of dharma. Then the final event that no man escapes brought me here." He gestured broadly with his hands. "You were kind enough to provide me with those ordinances I needed to progress. But, as you can see, I could not break away from that which I had striven to understand so desperately in my youth. The eightfold path proved but a partial solution, but I was unable to see beyond it."

"I'm still not sure I understand," I said wrinkling my brow.

"There were many great teachers—prophets. Buddha, Mohammed, Jesus. And while intellectually I know that Jesus was greater than the others and bow my knee to him, I still cannot forget the great teachings of Buddha to whom I still bow in reverence. Still, I am happy here. It is a wonderful kingdom—more marvelous than I had ever believed Nirvana to be."

He stopped and smiled again. "But, I have taken too much of your time." He rose and extended his hand again. "Thank you, Mark, for your selfless service. It exemplified two of the noble eightfold teachings—right action and right mindfulness. I just wanted to express my gratitude to you while you were here."

"Are you sure you would not like to accompany me?" I asked.

"Oh, no. I could not stand the eternal burning."

"I don't understand," I replied.

"You will." Gently he led me to the front of the Hall of Fame, turned, and walked down one of the roads that led away. Before he entered one of the buildings, he turned, smiled, and waved to me. I returned the wave. I wonder why he thanked me? It appears I did nothing for him.

I felt a gentle hand on my shoulder. The Guide stood beside me. "Are you ready to go?"

"I suppose," I said with a nod of my head.

"There is no rush," He replied, "if you'd like to stay longer."

"I don't suppose I've seen much at all. But if you are ready to leave, I'm ready to follow."

He smiled at me. "I know, Mark. You always have been." He gathered His robe around Him and we walked through the archway of the city. After we had walked for some distance I turned to look at its towers. They shone with a brilliant light against the surrounding darkness.

"What a wonderful, peaceful place," I exclaimed.

"Yes, it is. And those who dwell there are very happy people who are engaged in many good causes."

I turned back on the path and squinted my eyes as we approached something that glowed brighter than the sun.

Chapter 10

I covered my eyes with my hands and yet the brightness was so intense that I could see the bones in my fingers as if I were viewing a brightly colored X-ray. The Guide took my elbow in His hand and guided me to a personage standing at the side of the path.

"I'll leave you here, for a moment," He said. "The sentinels would like to ask you a few questions."

I felt His gentle grasp release my arm. The figure before me took my hand in his while I kept my other hand clamped across my eyes. Once the first sentinel had finished with me he led me to the second. When I finished with the fourth, the Guide took my arm again. My eyes had not adjusted to the intensity of the light, and I relied upon Him completely to guide me down the path.

The light was brighter than the noonday sun and I felt as if I would wither in its rays when the Guide stopped. "Lower your hands at your side, Mark," he said in a still, small voice.

I tried to remove my hands from before my face, but the light was so intense that I found it hard to comply with the Guide's request.

"Have faith, Mark," He said gently. "All will be well with you."

I took a deep breath and hung my hands down.

"Be still," the Guide said, and I felt His hands and

fingers rest on my face. Slowly He placed a finger on each eyelid. Whether my tolerance for light increased or the intensity decreased, I cannot say, but as He removed his hands from my face I blinked my eyes open in time to see the wounds in His hands.

I sank to my knees and bathed His feet in tears. "Oh Lord, my God," I wept.

Gently He reached down and raised me to my feet and embraced me.

"I am not worthy, Lord," I cried out in agony. "I am far from perfect."

His piercing eyes searched my face. "Mark, listen to me. Were you not a just man?"

"Just?"

Slowly He nodded his head. "Yes, Mark, a just man made perfect through the shedding of my blood."

"But I never served in any position of authority. I was just a teacher."

"So was I," He said with a smile. "It matters not where you serve, but how." He reached out for my arm and turned me toward the gates of the city. They seemed to be encircled with flames of fire. He led me past the other sentinels who stood guard at the city gates, and through the portal into the city.

"There are several who have been waiting for you, Mark," He said gently as we stepped onto the streets of gold. "But before I take you to them, I must spend a few moments here," He gestured with his hands. "Please feel free to go wherever you'd like. When I've accomplished what I have to do, I'll find you."

"There are so many!" I exclaimed. "More than I expected."

"All are welcome, Mark. My Father and I wanted everyone to return, why else would I have gone through the agony of Gethsemane and Calvary? But there can be no force, only free will. All must make their own choice. Do you understand?"

I nodded my head and He turned and walked quickly toward a cluster of people who were standing just inside the gate. My heart swelled with love within me as I watched Him go. I stood rooted to the spot taking in the beauty and glory of this kingdom, when I felt a gentle hand on my shoulder and, turning, I saw a magnificent man smiling at me.

"Welcome, Mark," he said simply. "Your talents are sorely needed here." He extended his hand and took mine in it. "My name is Alvin," he said with a smile. "I heard you were coming and I'm so pleased you are here. There is much work to do, and you have talents uniquely suited to our needs."

"I'll do whatever is needed," I replied.

"I know you will," he said, still smiling, "That's what makes you so valuable."

"Would you think me rude if I asked what it is you need me to do?"

"Not at all. I've been given charge of teaching those who came here without having heard our message, but whom we know will accept it. They would have accepted it in the other place, had they heard it." He continued to smile, "Does that make sense? It is a rather unique situation."

I nodded my head and asked, "Are there many of them?"

Alvin turned toward the city and opened his arms expansively. "Very many. And we have the opportunity to teach them all." He turned back to me. "That is why you are so valuable to us—to them."

"As I said, I'd be happy to do whatever is needed."

Alvin nodded his head. "After you get settled, we'll make arrangements for you to visit with us and learn your assignment."

"Am I not staying here?" I asked.

He smiled again and shook his head gently. "I think you are headed there," and he pointed at the glowing peak that arose behind the city. "Mount Zion."

"I'm confused," I stammered.

"It will all make sense in due time," he replied. "Ah, the Master approaches." He bowed as the white-clad figure walked to my side.

"You've met Alvin, I see."

"Yes. He says he has need of me."

"Yes, we do. And I know you will do well under his guidance. He has a legion of helpers whom you will learn to love. But, come, we have yet another stop to make before we reach our destination." He walked purposefully up the golden-paved street toward the towering mountain. After we had walked a considerable distance past beautiful buildings and well-appointed parks and gardens bursting with blossoms, we reached a stairway that glowed like amber lighted from within. The ever-present sentinels stood upon the steps and each bowed as we approached.

At the top of the long staircase an even more splendid

view expanded before me. The buildings were even more brilliant and glorious than those in the lower city, the gardens filled with trees and shrubbery bordered with flowers of every hue imaginable. The beauty took my breath away. There were people moving through the parks, each surrounded with a glow that illuminated the pathways as they walked.

"I've never seen such beauty," I whispered.

"It is glorious, isn't it? These people work very hard to make this a peaceful, beautiful place in which to live while they wait."

"Wait?"

"For their ordinances to be done," he said simply. "Baptism opens the door, but unless they enter into the new and everlasting covenant, they cannot walk through it to dwell with my Father on Mount Zion."

"They must be frustrated," I said.

"To some extent," he replied. "But the work will be done and this is a very pleasant place to dwell."

I nodded my head in agreement. "I've never seen anything like it. I have no words to describe its beauty."

The men and women who passed us each smiled and bowed in respect to my Guide.

"They seem very happy."

"They are the fruits of Alvin's labors. He and the other teachers do a wonderful job and I'm sure they will be glad to have your skills added to theirs."

"Who are these people?" I asked.

"My friends," he simply replied with a smile.

We walked on through orchards and vineyards drawing closer to Mount Zion. The gold-paved road was bordered with brilliant colored flowers whose perfume filled the air. I had never felt so peaceful in my life.

"What have I done to deserve this?" I said in amazement. "I accomplished nothing noteworthy in life."

The Master looked at me. "Greater love has no man than to lay down his life for his friends."

"I don't understand," I said with a puzzled look on my face. "I didn't lay down my life."

"Didn't you? You gave a life of service to others, Mark. Think back—put aside false modesty—didn't you pass up many of the pleasures of life to continue in your profession? It was not rich in material rewards, but it allowed you to influence the lives of thousands. Your neighbor, Sister Maxfield, who never married—didn't you weed her garden and shovel her walks? Weren't you always willing to help your quorum with service projects?" He took my hands in His. "Of course you did, Mark, and when you have done it for the least of these, you have done it for me."

"But everyone does those things," I said shaking my head.

"Not all and not willingly," he replied. His eyes searched my face, "And few have gone through the refiner's fire, as you did."

"I'm not sure what you mean."

"You lost your wife and daughter to a foolish drunken driver and still remained faithful in the face of that adversity. Many men would have cursed God. But your faith never wavered." He placed his hands on my shoulders, "Mark, you are a remarkable, humble man who is truly pure of heart." He smiled at me. "But come, there is still more for you to see."

We had reached the foothills of the mountain and had begun to climb a winding trail that led to the top. At a switchback I looked out over the valley below. I could see the lower city where Alvin labored and the upper one with its inhabitants who waited patiently. The mountain loomed above us.

Chapter 11

As we approached the top of the peak I noticed the light was growing brighter. And then I heard the sound of children's laughter.

"It is a most pleasant sound," the Guide said as if he read my mind.

"Yes, it is," I agreed. "I didn't realize how much I missed it. I heard none of it in the other places I visited."

"No. It is only here that families dwell."

We reached the top of the mountain and found a city surrounded by an artistically carved wall. It glowed as with an inner light. The Guide led me to a recessed door and knocked. He paused then knocked twice more. From within a voice responded, "Yes?"

"Father, I have brought Mark to the door. He is worthy to enter."

The voice from beyond the door penetrated to the very core of my soul. He questioned me as to my readiness and then, apparently satisfied, opened the door and extended his hand to me. He drew me through the door.

"Father," said the Guide, "here is a man without guile."

"Welcome." He embraced me. "There are many people waiting to greet you." He extended his hand toward a palace that rose at the far end of the amber streets.

We walked toward the building and I could see a throng of people standing on the steps. Suddenly two of them broke from the crowd and raced down the street to meet us. I recognized my dear, sweet wife and our daughter and ran to meet them. I gathered them in my arms and kissed them as we wept together.

"My darling," I whispered as the tears flowed freely. "I've missed you so much."

She hugged me tightly and said, "And I have missed you. But I'm all right and it's all true."

I knelt, hugged my daughter, and wept tears of joy. I felt a hand on my shoulder and looked up into the face of my Father.

"When you are finished, there are others waiting to greet you." He smiled and gestured toward the steps.

I held my wife's and daughter's hands in mine and we walked toward the palace. I could see two glowing thrones, seemingly encircled with fire, through the open door at the top of the flight of stairs. As we approached the steps I began to recognize many of my family who had gone before and, as I recognized them, they left the steps and walked toward us for a glorious reunion.

The Guide spoke quietly. "You do not recognize the others?" He said gesturing toward the crowd left on the steps.

I shook my head. "No. Should I?"

"They are those whom Alvin's teachers helped to learn of my Father and me and for whom you performed their ordinances in the temple. They are those for whom you have become a savior on Mount Zion."

Upon hearing those words the crowd left the steps and surrounded us.

After several minutes the Guide said in His quiet voice,

"This has been a wonderful reunion, but we are very busy here. There is much work to be done. If your wife will show you to your mansion, I'd like to take you down to meet with Alvin. He needs your skills."

"Mansion?" I asked in surprise. "A simple house would be sufficient."

He smiled and said, "In my Father's house are many mansions. I have prepared a place for you. My Father has given me all that He has and you are my joint heir." He nodded to my wife and she gently led me away from the people who were beginning to disperse and return to their labors.

"When you are ready, Mark," the Guide said, "I will be ready, too." He smiled His gentle smile and watched me walk away with my wife and daughter. He and His Father then climbed the steps of the palace toward their burning thrones.

The three of us walked down a gold-paved street toward an expansive home surrounded by perfectly proportioned shrubs and flowers. Fountains played on each side of the walk as we stepped through the archway that led to the front door.

"Welcome home," my wife said, squeezing my hand.

My daughter pulled my face down to hers and kissed me. "Welcome home, father."

And at that minute I knew that, truly, I was home.

About the Author

Richard M. Siddoway was born in Salt Lake City and raised in Bountiful, Utah. He has been a professional educator for over 40 years. Currently he is the Principal of the Electronic High School.

He served three terms in the Utah House of Representatives and is currently the President of the Bountiful, Utah Stake. He and his wife, Janice, have eight children and 16 grandchildren (with 17 and 18 on the way).

He is the author of *Twelve Tales of Christmas, Mom and Other Great Women I Have Known, Habits of the Heart, The Hut in the Tree in the Woods, Christmas of the Cherry Snow, The Christmas Quest,* and the New York Times bestseller, *The Christmas Wish.*